HOW TO BE BRAVE

by
Nancy Wilcox Richards

illustrations by
Mathieu Benoit

Scholastic Canada Ltd.
Toronto New York London Auckland Sydney
Mexico City New Delhi Hong Kong Buenos Aires

Scholastic Canada Ltd.
604 King Street West, Toronto, Ontario M5V 1E1, Canada

Scholastic Inc.
557 Broadway, New York, NY 10012, USA

Scholastic Australia Pty Limited
PO Box 579, Gosford, NSW 2250, Australia

Scholastic New Zealand Limited
Private Bag 94407, Botany, Manukau 2163, New Zealand

Scholastic Children's Books
Euston House, 24 Eversholt Street, London NW1 1DB, UK

www.scholastic.ca

Library and Archives Canada Cataloguing in Publication

Richards, Nancy Wilcox, 1958-, author
How to be brave / Nancy Wilcox Richards ; illustrated
by Mathieu Benoit.

ISBN 978-1-4431-5800-8 (softcover)

I. Benoit, Mathieu, 1978-, illustrator II. Title.

PS8585.I184H6717 2017   jC813'.54   C2017-901498-6

6 5 4 3 2 1   Printed in Canada 121   17 18 19 20 21

MIX
Paper from
responsible sources
FSC® C004071

For all those kids who show bravery in many ways, especially my "kids," Jenn and Kris

— N.W.R.

Chapter 1

Daniel Couture really liked being the older brother. Even though it was only by seven minutes, he was still older than his twin sister, Fiona. They might have been born in the same hospital, on the same day, and weighed exactly the same amount, but they weren't anything alike.

Fiona thought summer was the best time of the year. She loved swimming in the deep end of the pool — especially after cannonballing off the diving board. Daniel wished it could be winter forever. That way he could snowboard all year long — zipping down hills that seemed as tall as mountains.

In his spare time, Daniel loved playing his

guitar — rock 'n' roll, country, blues. When Fiona had free time, she liked to watch TV. Cartoons and spooky movies — the scarier the better.

When the Couture family moved to their new house, Fiona decided that she didn't need to sleep with a night light anymore. Daniel tried to do the same thing. But the new place made weird sounds — especially at night. The radiators groaned and the plumbing creaked. Mom said it was part of the old house's charm. Daniel thought it was kind of creepy. Plus every night when he was almost asleep, he was sure he heard strange noises coming from his closet. Then he'd jump out of bed and flick on his night light.

No one in his family seemed to care that he wasn't quite as brave as Fiona. Mom was always saying to give new things a try. She said that if Daniel was willing to do that, it was a first step toward being brave. Mom was usually right. Like the first time she had cooked fiddleheads. Daniel had eyed the green vegetables suspiciously. He took one sniff. He thought fiddleheads smelled a lot like freshly cut grass.

"I think I'd like to have more potatoes instead," he said.

But Fiona scooped a humongous forkful of fiddleheads into her mouth and declared, "These are delicious!"

"Really?" asked Daniel. He picked up a fiddlehead and nibbled a teeny tiny bite. His sister was right. Fiddleheads *were* delicious! Ever since, fiddleheads were one of his favourite veggies — right after potatoes and corn.

He had eaten that first dish of fiddleheads in Grade One. That was a long time ago. And trying new foods wasn't the same as swimming in the deep end of the pool or joining Scouts. Trying new stuff was hard.

That's why being brave was all he'd wanted since his eighth birthday.

Three years ago, when Daniel and Fiona turned six, they had blown out the candles on their birthday cake together. Both of them had wished for brand new bikes. That was exactly what they got for their birthday that year.

When they turned seven, Fiona had wished for a magician's kit. When she unwrapped her gift, it was a beginner's magic set. Daniel had wished for a kitten. That very day the whole family went to the animal shelter and Daniel got to pick out whichever kitten he wanted. There were short-haired cats and long-haired cats. There were cuddly cats and cats with attitude. Daniel chose a black kitten with snow-white paws. Mittens had been part of the family ever since.

Now there wasn't much time left until their ninth birthday. Daniel was disappointed that last year's birthday wish hadn't come true yet. He was starting to think it probably wasn't going to happen. When Daniel blew out the candles, he had even crossed his fingers. On both hands. *I want to be brave like Fiona*, he wished.

He hoped he wouldn't have to wait too much longer. Because even though it was April and the school year was almost over, tomorrow he was starting at a new school — River Haven Elementary. He really needed to feel brave when he met all the new kids in his class, plus a new teacher.

Maybe by morning, he thought, *my wish will have come true.*

Chapter 2

That evening Daniel filled his backpack: one package of pencils, a box of smelly markers, two erasers, his favourite gym sneakers and lots of report folders. The backpack had glow-in-the-dark stripes, but the best part was the secret compartment on the inside.

He looked over at Fiona. She was busy labelling her folders. "I'm going to miss my old friends," he said. "What if the kids are mean?" His eyes grew wide. "What if the teacher is boring or yells a lot or gives too much homework?" He groaned. "What if we're not in the same class?"

Daniel and Fiona had been in the same class ever since nursery school. Whenever Daniel felt nervous or afraid, Fiona had always been there, reminding him that things were okay. If he felt too shy to answer the teacher, Fiona would do it for him.

"We'll probably be in the same class," Fiona said. "We always are. But if we're not, I'll still see you at recess and lunchtime."

That night Daniel had a hard time falling asleep. He thought about counting sheep, but that was pretty boring. He thought about unpacking his school supplies and repacking them again, just to make sure he had everything he needed. But his backpack was by the front door and he didn't want Mom or Dad quizzing him about why he was still awake. Instead he tossed and turned in his bed. He fluffed his pillows. He threw the covers off and, a few minutes later, pulled them up under his chin. He wondered if Fiona was fast asleep in her room. *Probably*, he thought. Fiona wasn't scared to go to a new school. She wasn't afraid to make new friends. She was Fearless Fiona.

Chapter 3

The next morning Dad drove Daniel and Fiona to River Haven Elementary. "You can start taking the bus tomorrow," he said. "But for today, just to make sure that you are both settled, I'll drive you."

River Haven Elementary was humongous. It reminded Daniel of a castle, a really old castle.

"Wow," gushed Fiona. "That is the coolest building!"

Daniel stared at the school. He felt like there were dozens of butterflies in his belly. A kid could get lost in a school that big. Maybe he wouldn't be found for hours. Or days. Maybe never. He thought about his old school — small, with only four classrooms. Already he missed it.

"Okay, kiddos," said Dad. "Let's go meet your new teacher."

Ms. Belliveau was sitting at her computer when they entered the room.

"You must be Daniel and Fiona," she said. "I've been expecting the two of you. Welcome to River Haven Elementary and your new Grade Three class."

Sweet! thought Daniel. *Fiona and I are in the same class!*

Ms. Belliveau stood up.

"Let's get you two settled," she said. "Daniel, you'll sit here." Ms. Belliveau pointed to an empty desk. "Right next to Andrew. And Fiona, you'll be sitting over there, next to Madison." She pointed to a desk on the other side of the room.

Daniel unpacked his school supplies and stowed them in his desk.

"Time for me to go," announced Dad. "You two have a great day."

Fiona stopped organizing her folders. She ran over and hugged Dad goodbye.

Daniel watched. Dad was leaving. Soon it would be just him and Fiona. Plus a whole roomful of kids he didn't know. He took a deep breath and exhaled. His eyes burned and he swallowed hard.

He was just about to give Dad a goodbye hug when the bell rang. A boy raced into the classroom. He was really big. He looked like he should be in Grade Four. Maybe even Grade Five. Daniel hung back. He eyed the boy carefully. Should he still hug Dad? Or would this big kid think that only babies hugged their parents? He wished he was brave enough to do exactly what he wanted and not worry about what another kid thought. But he wasn't.

Daniel lowered his eyes and pretended to look for something in his desk. "See you later, Dad," he mumbled.

Dad waved goodbye. "I'll pick you up at bell time. Have a great day!"

Chapter 4

Daniel sat at his new desk. He watched kids file into the room. He wondered which one was Andrew. But more importantly, he wondered if he'd be nice.

He didn't have to wait long. A skinny boy wearing glasses slid into the seat next to him. He smiled at Daniel. "You must be the new kid," he said. He had a tooth missing in exactly the same spot as Daniel.

Daniel nodded.

Ms. Belliveau walked over. She smiled at Daniel. "I see you've met Andrew," she said. "He's going to take you and your sister on a tour of the school." She looked at Andrew. "But before he does that, here are a few 'icebreaker questions.' They might help you to get to know each other." Ms. Belliveau handed Andrew a set of cards.

"Some of the questions on the cards are kind of cool," Andrew explained to Fiona and Daniel. "Some of them are kind of boring. But Ms. Belliveau does this whenever we get a new kid or meet other kids in the school — like our reading buddies from Grade Five."

Andrew looked at the first card. "They're supposed to be short answers. And quick. So just say the first thing that you think of. Here we go. The first category is called 'Favourite Things.' Ready? Vanilla or chocolate?"

"Chocolate," answered Daniel.

"Vanilla," said Fiona.

"Colour?"

"Red."

"Purple."

"Hamburgers or hot dogs?"

"Hot dogs!" they both answered.

The next categories were about family, vacations and school. When Fiona answered the last question, Andrew handed her the cards. "Now it's your turn," he explained.

"The category is called 'Numbers,'" she said. Then she read, "Teeth lost."

"Eight."

"Brothers or sisters?"

When Andrew answered, "Almost one," Fiona laughed.

"What do you mean?" she asked.

So Andrew explained that he didn't have any brothers or sisters — yet. "But my mom is going to have a baby pretty soon. Her belly looks like she swallowed a beach ball!" He giggled. "So I have either a brother or a sister. Just not born yet."

Fiona nodded. Now his answer made perfect sense.

"Phone number?" read Daniel.

Fiona and Daniel took turns asking questions. When they were finished, they started the tour of River Haven Elementary. The three of them walked out into a hallway that twisted and curved out of sight. Andrew pointed to the left. "Down that way is the other Grade Three class." He pointed to the right. "That's how you get to the Grade Two rooms. But first I'll show you where the gym is. That's the best part about school."

It seemed like they walked around in circles, through a bazillion doors. "Here's the gym," he said. "And past that is the cafeteria."

Fiona's eyes were huge. "This place is humongous," she said. "And it's so neat!"

"And old," added Andrew. "My mom went to this school when she was little. She got lost once. She couldn't figure out how to get back to her classroom from the basement."

"What was she doing in the basement?" Daniel asked.

Andrew laughed. "Not much. Just looking for the caretaker. That's where his workroom is."

Fiona glanced at Daniel. He knew exactly what she was thinking. Sometimes she didn't even have to say a word. Daniel knew she was thinking the same thing as him: River Haven *was* really big. It would be easy to get lost.

After seeing the library, the principal's office and the music room, Andrew pointed to a set of stairs. "Those go to the basement," he said. "There's nothing much down there. Just the caretaker's room, a bunch of ladders and old stuff."

"And maybe a missing kid from a hundred years ago," laughed Daniel. Andrew and Fiona laughed, too.

Chapter 5

There were lots of things to do at lunchtime. Some kids played on the outdoor equipment, like the swings or the teeter-totters. Some played games like four-square or skipped rope. Others belonged to clubs — Arts and Crafts, Basketball or Recycling.

Daniel sat with Fiona in the cafeteria. He nibbled the last little bit of his lunch. Dad had packed his favourite dessert — chocolate-covered raisins.

He shoved a handful into his mouth as he watched Andrew pack up part of a leftover sandwich and a few celery sticks.

"Do you want to join a club?" Andrew asked. "It's every Monday at lunchtime, twelve thirty to one. It's tons of fun!"

Daniel thought about the Guitar Club at his old school. There had been only eight kids in the club, and Daniel had been the youngest. It was the best thing ever. The club met after school twice a week. It was the reason he started playing guitar.

"Is it a Guitar Club?" he asked hopefully.

"Nah. We don't have a Guitar Club. It's called the Kids 4 Comedy Club. We meet today." He glanced at his watch. "In ten minutes."

Daniel stared at Andrew. He wasn't exactly sure what "comedy" meant. "What do you do in the club?" he asked.

Andrew explained that the club was all about jokes and fun stuff. Sometimes the kids traded books on riddles. Sometimes they watched a funny video. "The only thing you have to do is tell a joke or riddle each week," he said.

"You mean in front of people?" Daniel asked.

"Well," he said, "you just tell the joke to the kids in the club. It's not like you have to do it in front of the entire school or anything like that."

Daniel swallowed hard. There was no way

he wanted to get up and speak in front of a
whole bunch of kids, even if it *was* a fun club
to belong to. Sure, he'd love to hear the jokes,
maybe even solve a riddle. He was good at
that. But to have to tell his own joke? Just
the thought of it made his hands sweaty.

"Sounds like fun," he said. He looked down
at the table. "But maybe another time. I want
to check out the playground. Plus, I need
to finish my lunch." He held up his bag of
chocolate-covered raisins and began to eat
them slowly, one by one.

"Can I join?" Fiona asked. "I know a joke I
could tell today!"

With that, Fiona threw the rest of her lunch

in her lunch bag. As she walked out the cafeteria doors, Daniel heard her say, "Have you heard the joke about the elephant and the monkey?"

Daniel sighed. Fiona certainly wasn't shy. She never worried about stuff like telling a joke to a bunch of kids, even if she didn't know the kids very well. In fact, she loved meeting new people. Some day, if his birthday wish ever came true, Daniel would actually enjoy meeting new kids. He'd be brave enough to tell jokes at the Kids 4 Comedy Club — maybe even the whole school. Just not today.

Chapter 6

Supper that night was Daniel's favourite — spaghetti with lots of meatballs. He slurped his noodles.

"So," began Mom, "tell me about your first day at River Haven." She glanced from Daniel to Fiona.

"The school is really cool," began Fiona. "There are winding halls and old cloakrooms. There's even a basement. Some kids disappear when they go down there!"

Mom dropped her fork and stared at Fiona. "Disappear? What do you mean?"

Fiona laughed. "Well, they don't *actually* disappear. But a long time ago, a kid couldn't find her way out of the basement. The teacher had to send someone looking for her."

Daniel stared at his sister. He thought it sounded kind of farfetched that someone could actually disappear in a school.

"That reminds me of a riddle," he said. "What disappears every time you stand up?"

Mom thought. Dad thought and thought. Fiona scratched her head, repeating, "What disappears every time you stand up?"

When everyone had given up, Daniel answered, "Your lap!"

Fiona laughed. Daniel was great at riddles, especially solving them. "You could have told that one at the Comedy Club today," she said. When Daniel didn't say anything, she continued. "Anyway . . . I think I'm really going to like our new school," she said. "It's *waaaay* more exciting than our old school."

Mom laughed. "It sounds like you enjoyed your first day." She looked over at Daniel. "What about you?" she asked. "How was your day?"

Daniel looked down at his plate. What could he say? Ms. Belliveau seemed okay. The work had been easy. But the school was big. Really big. He was sure he'd get lost once he set foot outside of the classroom.

Daniel chose his words carefully. "My day was pretty good. I made a new friend. His name is Andrew and he seems nice."

Dad smiled. "That's great!" he said. "Maybe Andrew can come over some day after school. You could even invite him to your birthday party next month."

Just the mention of the words "birthday party" reminded Daniel that his wish hadn't come true. He hadn't felt the least bit brave today. Not when he was meeting new kids or joining activities or finding his way around his new school.

Chapter 7

"Class," began Ms. Belliveau, "today we are starting our unit on plant and animal habitats. Does anyone know what a habitat is?" She looked around the room. A few hands went up.

"Yes, Madison," said Ms. Belliveau. "What do you think it is?"

"I think it's something an animal does over and over again," she guessed.

Someone at the back of the room snickered.

Ms. Belliveau shook her head and smiled. "Good try. It sounds like you're thinking about the word 'habit.' Anyone else?"

Daniel was about to raise his hand. He was almost positive that a habitat was where an animal lived. But maybe that was wrong.

And what if someone snickered at his wrong answer just like they had at Madison's? *I better not answer*, he thought.

"It's a place where living things live," shouted a voice from the back of the room.

Ms. Belliveau nodded her head. "Yes! Today we will look at habitats in our outdoor classroom." Then she held up a hula hoop. "You and your partner will need one of these, your science journal and a pencil. I'd like you to place the hula hoop in only one area — one habitat — of the outdoor classroom. Draw a sketch of the kinds of animals you see inside the hoop. Record how many you see. If you know its name, jot that down, too. If you don't know its name, you can use the class camera to take a picture. Then you can research it once we get back to the classroom."

Andrew leaned over and whispered to Daniel, "Let's be partners."

Daniel smiled. That sounded like a great plan.

Outside, Andrew placed the hula hoop in

the farthest corner of the outdoor classroom, near a small pond. "I think this will be a good spot," he said. "How about I turn over this rock and you check what's under it?"

Daniel nodded. "Sure!"

Carefully Andrew lifted the rock. Tiny black bugs scurried away in all directions.

Daniel recorded the word "ants" in his journal. Then he wrote, "Moved too fast to count." He glanced up from his paper. "Did you know that ants have two stomachs?" he asked Andrew.

Andrew laughed. "Really?"

"Yup," answered Daniel. "One is for its own food. The other is for food to share with other ants."

"Eww," said Andrew. "That's gross! What do the other ants do — eat throw-up?"

Daniel laughed. "Pretty much," he answered. Then he pointed. "Look at that!"

Climbing up the side of the rock was something small and brown. Daniel added the words "one slug" to his journal.

"Do you know what that is?" asked Andrew. He pointed to a small blackish-brown bug with lines across its back. He touched it and the bug curled into a ball. "It reminds me of an armadillo."

"Nope," answered Daniel. "Let's take a picture. We can figure it out when we go inside. I'll get the camera from Ms. Belliveau."

A few minutes later, Daniel came back with the camera. He took a picture.

Then he and Andrew searched the grass inside the hula hoop. They didn't find any more bugs. So they waited. And waited. And waited.

It was boring with nothing to count but blades of grass and weeds. Then suddenly they heard a loud scream. It sounded like something terrible had happened.

Chapter 8

Daniel watched Ms. Belliveau race over to a crying Madison. His sister was waving her hands in the air like she was trying to explain something. Ms. Belliveau went from looking worried to looking unhappy. A group of kids stood nearby. Some looked sympathetic. But a few of them looked like they were trying really hard not to laugh.

"It's okay, boys and girls. Everyone can go back to work. It was just a little misunderstanding," Ms. Belliveau said. Then she turned and said something to Fiona in a low voice. Fiona hung her head.

Something was definitely wrong.

When science class was over, Daniel fell in line next to Fiona. They walked back into the school. "What happened?" he whispered. "Ms. Belliveau looked really mad at you."

"Madison lied to me! That's what happened!" Fiona said. "She said she wasn't afraid of bugs. That she picked them up all the time. But when I put a teeny tiny cricket on her arm, she started screaming. Now she's mad at me and so is the teacher."

Daniel was quiet for a minute. "I guess sometimes people say stuff that's not really true."

Fiona nodded. "Did you find anything really interesting in your hula hoop?"

"A bunch of ants, a slug and a bug we didn't know the name of," he answered. "Andrew and I are going to look it up on the internet."

As soon as they were in the classroom, Daniel looked up "bugs that curl into a ball." A picture that perfectly matched the photo he had taken popped up on the computer screen.

"It's a pill bug!" Andrew exclaimed. "Also known as a roly poly." He continued to read. "A pill bug is not an insect. It belongs to the crustacean family — the same group as lobsters and crabs. It can roll into a complete ball to protect itself."

Daniel recorded "roly poly" in his journal. He scrunched up his face. "Ewww," he said, reading from the screen. "It says pill bugs eat their own scat. Doesn't that mean poop? Gross."

Andrew laughed. "I think so," he said. "And look! It says their blood is blue! If it gets sick, the pill bug turns a bright blue colour."

Just then Ms. Belliveau called the class to the Meeting Corner.

"I saw lots of ants!" someone called out.

"I found a cricket!"

"I found a salamander!"

"Spiders!"

"A beetle!"

Ms. Belliveau recorded each answer. "There

certainly were lots of different animals," she said. "Now, I'd like you to think about which animal you'd like to research. Each one of you will give a presentation. Your  presentation can be on any of the animals we found today. Choose one you'd like to learn more about."

"I'm going to pick the salamander," Andrew said. "What are you going to research, Daniel?"

Daniel didn't answer. He was too busy thinking about the words Ms. Belliveau had said. Everyone had to give a presentation. Just the thought of getting up in front of the class — with a bunch of kids he hardly knew — made his hands sweaty and his heart race. The one thing he feared more than anything in the whole wide world was giving presentations.

Chapter 9

When Ms. Belliveau announced that the class would be going on a field trip, everyone was excited! There would be a real dinosaur skeleton, a ninety-year-old tortoise and a bug display at the Museum of Natural History.

"And there is a whole new section at the museum called Creepy Crawlies," said Ms. Belliveau. "There will be bees, salamanders and spiders. It fits in perfectly with our work on animals and their habitats. You might even learn some new information for your presentation."

Daniel thought it sounded like fun — except for the presentation part. He thought of Fiona. She loved to talk to big groups of people. A presentation would be no big deal for her. The last time she had given one, she told Daniel that it made her feel important. Kind of like an expert.

Fiona studied her brother's worried face. "You know, it won't be like in Grade Two," she said. "I'll help you rehearse."

Daniel remembered his Grade Two presentation like it had happened yesterday. Actually, it was more like he had *tried* to give his presentation. It was on his favourite sport, snowboarding. He had practised his speech. He had a poster showing some of the tricks he could do on his board. But when he stood in front of the whole class, his mouth got dry and his belly started to roll. When he opened his mouth to speak, only a squeak came out. Then a hiccup. Everyone laughed so hard, he couldn't even remember how to start his talk. So he just stood there feeling embarrassed. Finally, his teacher said he looked like he didn't feel well and let him sit out the rest of the class. That had been the last day for presentations before March Break. When they got back after their vacation, they moved on to other things and he never did have to give his presentation.

"I have a plan to help you," Fiona told him.

"I don't think anything will help," said Daniel. "You actually like giving presentations. You're not afraid of doing that."

That evening, after supper, Fiona handed Daniel a piece of paper. "These are tips for your presentation," she said.

Daniel read the tips:

Don't be boring!
Practise talking in front of a mirror.
Pee before you give your talk.
Use a prop.
Picture the whole class in their underwear!

Daniel thought about picturing all the kids in their underwear and laughed out loud. "Do you really do that, Fiona?"

"Sometimes," she admitted. "It helps to take away the butterflies in my belly. And it makes me feel like I am in charge."

Chapter 10

When Daniel woke up the next morning, he was grumpy. He didn't want his usual breakfast — peanut butter and jelly on toast. The shirt he was going to wear had mud on the sleeve. And he dropped his favourite Lego man down the drain.

Mom took one look at his face and said, "Someone's a little cranky this morning."

"*Humph*," Daniel replied.

Daniel had tossed and turned all night long. He had almost fallen asleep when he heard something in his closet. Again. After that, he turned on his night light. But it was hard to fall asleep — especially while keeping an eye on the closet *and* thinking about giving his presentation. When he did finally fall asleep, he dreamt he was in front of the class giving a presentation, wearing nothing except his underwear. Kids were laughing at him. Even Ms. Belliveau couldn't hide her big smile. To make matters worse, Daniel started to cry — right in front of everyone. And he knew it was all because of Fiona's "helpful tips."

Fiona studied Daniel carefully. "What's the matter?" she asked.

"*You're* what's the matter," he grumbled. "Your tips are terrible! I couldn't fall asleep, and when I did, I had bad dreams all night. I dreamt I gave my presentation in my underwear!"

Fiona scrunched her eyebrows together and frowned. "I was only trying to help!" she said.

"Well, I don't need that kind of help!" Daniel scowled at his sister.

Mom stepped between the two of them. "That's enough," she said, "from both of you. Get ready for school."

Daniel glared at his sister. She glared back.

"Baby," she whispered, just low enough that Mom couldn't hear.

* * *

Things went from bad to worse at school. Daniel made so many mistakes on his math sheet that he had to redo almost the entire page. That meant he was late getting outside for recess. Gym was cancelled because they had to listen to a presentation. And it was B-O-R-I-N-G. Boring. During art, he cut his finger when he was using his scissors. He tried not to cry, but it hurt too much. Not even the bandage helped.

But the worst thing was, halfway through

his art project, he spilled red paint on Ms. Belliveau's shoes. It spread over the floor, looking like a puddle of blood. Even though Ms. Belliveau said it was all right and she knew it was an accident, she looked upset.

"Daniel," she sighed, "please go down to the basement and ask the janitor if he could come to our room with some cleaning supplies."

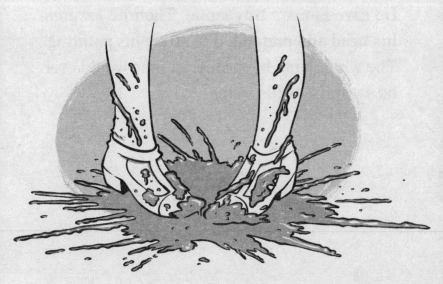

Daniel thought the basement was spooky. Plus, he remembered the story about Andrew's mother getting lost. What if *he* couldn't find his way back to the classroom? He looked up at Ms. Belliveau. She was expecting him to go. Maybe he should just be honest and say he wasn't sure of the way.

Fiona jumped out of her seat. "I'll go!" she said. "That way Daniel can keep working on his painting. Mine is already finished." She held up her painting for Ms. Belliveau to see.

Fiona glanced over at Daniel's relieved face. He gave Fiona a tiny smile. Then he lowered his head and pretended to study his painting. The whole time he wondered if he would ever be as brave as his sister.

Chapter 11

The class continued to work on their research projects. Every day, just before bell time, the kids shared a few facts they had learned.

Fiona went first. She explained that she was reading about dragonflies. So far she had learned that dragonflies have excellent eyesight and that they have been around for millions of years.

She laughed, "That's way older than Great-Grandma!"

The class laughed, too.

Andrew shared that his project was on salamanders. "Did you know that salamanders are nocturnal?" He paused. "That means they are more active at night. But the neatest fact I've learned is that salamanders can grow back missing tails and even their legs!"

Ms. Belliveau nodded. "That's very interesting, Andrew." She looked around the room. "Would anyone else like to share information? Daniel, how about you?"

Daniel looked at the huge stack of books on his desk. There were books about ladybugs. There were books about caterpillars and butterflies. He even had one on garter snakes.

"I haven't quite decided which animal I'd like to research," he admitted. "There are so many interesting ones." He could feel his face going red as he pointed to all the books heaped on his desk.

He thought about all the facts he had learned so far. It was cool to know that a male mosquito will never bite you; only the females bite. Now, if only he could figure out a way to tell the boy mosquitoes from the girl mosquitoes. He'd have it made!

And who knew that butterflies tasted with their feet? *What if humans did that?*

he thought. *Imagine tasting the inside of sweaty sneakers. Ewww, gross!*

Daniel already knew that garter snakes weren't dangerous, but he had read a few new facts about them — like they usually have twenty to forty babies at one time. That was a lot of little wriggly snakes!

The problem with reading so many

books, thought Daniel, *is that each animal is interesting. One minute I want to learn every possible fact about butterflies. The next minute I've changed my mind and I want to read about slugs.*

He sighed. How was he ever going to decide?

Chapter 12

On Friday both Daniel and Fiona came home from school with separate sleepover invitations. They sat at the kitchen table eating their snacks. Fiona licked some peanut butter from her finger.

"Madison invited me for a sleepover tonight," she told Mom. "She said we could make homemade pizza and watch scary movies! Can I go?"

Mom smiled at her. "Sure, if you'd like to. Her mom called me. It sounds like fun."

Daniel studied his glass of juice. He didn't look very happy. "I got an invitation for a sleepover, too," he said. "At Andrew's."

"That could be fun," said Mom. "Why the long face? Don't you want to go?"

Daniel sighed. He and Andrew were becoming good friends. And Mom was right — a sleepover *could* be fun. But he was still just trying to get used to sleeping in his own room. And he always slept with a night light. What would Andrew think about that? He'd probably think he was a baby, that's what. For the gazillionth time he wished he could be as brave as Fiona. She didn't need a night light anymore. She even liked to read scary books. No, that wasn't quite true. She *loved* to read scary books — the creepier the better.

"I'm not sure I want to go," he answered Mom. "I think I need to work on my animal project."

Fiona laughed. "Since when do you do homework on a Friday night?"

Daniel frowned at his sister.

Fiona finished the rest of her snack and headed to her room to pack an overnight bag for the sleepover. She picked out her favourite pyjamas — the ones that said "Dream Big" — her toothbrush, hairbrush, clean clothes for the next day and the book she was reading:

Zombie Invasion. She was almost finished packing when Daniel walked into her room. He didn't look very happy.

"You really should go to Andrew's for the sleepover," Fiona told him. "I bet you'd have a great time. You'll probably play with Lego and get to stay up really late."

Daniel hung his head. He scuffed the carpet with his toe. A sleepover *would* be lots of fun. He loved building with Lego. Maybe they could go biking before it got dark. He could even bring his telescope. Once the sun went down, he could show Andrew the craters on the moon. But he just didn't feel ready yet.

Chapter 13

Daniel and Dad were finishing breakfast the next morning when Fiona arrived home from Madison's sleepover. Her hair was a tangled mess and her T-shirt was on inside out.

Daniel laughed. "Your hair looks like a giant bird's nest," he said. "And you spilled something all over your pants." He pointed to a dark stain that looked like strawberry jam.

Fiona scowled at her brother. "I think you should mind your own business," she said crossly.

"Someone got up on the wrong side of the bed," said Dad as he poured coffee into his mug.

"That just shows what you know," answered Fiona. "I didn't even sleep in a bed. Madison and I made a fort out of blankets. We slept on the floor in the den." She stomped down the hallway to her bedroom.

Dad shook his head. "Well, that explains it."

Daniel knew that if Fiona stayed up past her bedtime, she was grouchy. She had probably stayed up too late and woken up extra early. *I better check and see how she's doing* he thought.

When he walked into her room, Fiona was stretched across her bed. Her eyes were closed. Mittens lay curled up next to her, licking her paws.

"You awake?" Daniel whispered.

Fiona opened one eye and stared at Daniel. "Sort of."

He plopped down on the side of her bed. "Didn't you have fun with Madison?"

At first Daniel thought maybe she hadn't heard him. Fiona just stared off into space. Finally she answered that yes, she had had fun.

"We each made our own pizzas. I put pepperoni, green peppers and extra cheese on mine," she said. "It was really yummy. We even got to make ice-cream sundaes for dessert. I had two helpings! But . . ." she paused. "I didn't sleep very well."

"Do you think you ate too much junk?" Daniel asked.

When Fiona didn't answer, he added, "Or maybe the floor was too hard to sleep on."

Fiona looked over at her brother. She shook her head. "It wasn't that the floor was too hard or that I pigged out on too much ice cream. We played lots of games and we even watched a movie. But . . ."

"But what?"

"I missed you. I missed Mom and Dad." She sniffed. She reached over and picked up Mittens. "I even missed this furball."

Daniel stared at Fiona. He could hardly believe what he was hearing. Fearless Fiona, who could pick up snakes and spiders, who wasn't afraid of getting lost in River Haven Elementary, hadn't been brave at a sleepover.

Chapter 14

The day of the class trip finally arrived. Daniel sat next to Andrew on the bus. He watched Ms. Belliveau count to make sure the entire class was on board. As the bus rolled out of the school driveway, Andrew turned to Daniel and said, "I hope we have time to visit Gus at the museum."

Daniel looked puzzled. "Gus? Who's Gus?"

"Gus is the ninety-year-old gopher tortoise who lives at the museum. Last time I got to feed him some lettuce. It was a lot of fun," Andrew explained.

"Cool," said Daniel. "Hey, I know a riddle about a tortoise. Do you want to hear it?" Before Andrew could respond, he blurted out, "How does a tortoise communicate?"

"I don't know," Andrew answered. "How does a tortoise communicate?"

"With a *shell*phone!"

"That's good. I'm going to tell that one at the Comedy Club next week," Andrew said. "Now, here's one for you: Why did the spider buy a computer?"

Daniel shook his head. He didn't know the answer to that riddle.

"Because he wanted a website!" Andrew nudged Daniel's arm. "Get it?"

When Ms. Belliveau announced they had arrived at the Museum of Natural History, the class was divided into small groups with chaperones. Daniel, Andrew, Fiona and Madison were all in the same group. Everyone was given a scavenger hunt sheet.

"Try to answer as many questions as you can," Ms. Belliveau instructed. "You will be able to figure out most things by looking at all the displays in the Creepy Crawlies section of the museum. The last clue will tell you where we'll meet for lunch. See you then — and remember to have fun!"

Daniel read the first question out loud: "What insect can fly up to fifty-six kilometres per hour?"

That was an easy one for the group to answer. Fiona spotted a sign near the dragonfly display. She read, "Dragonflies have been known to travel up to fifty-six kilometres per hour. The largest known dragonfly had a wingspan of one hundred centimetres." She paused. "That's as long as an entire metre stick!" she exclaimed. "That's really big!"

The next question was a little trickier. Madison read, "How many ant graveyards can you find?" She looked at Daniel, Andrew and Fiona. "I didn't know that ants have graveyards. Did you?"

It took quite a bit of time to answer that question. Next to the ant farm, Andrew read, "If you look closely at the far right-hand corner, you might see an ant graveyard. Two days after an ant has died, its body releases a smell. This smell alerts the rest of the ants that the dead carcass should be carted off and dumped into a pile with all the other dead ants. Yup — that's what we call the *ant graveyard!*"

"I guess that means there is only one graveyard," said Daniel.

The group quickly solved the next three clues in the scavenger hunt. Finally there was only one clue left to solve.

Daniel read: "Come have lunch with me. I'm a little tricky to see. Ten centimetres long with yellow spots. Find me beneath a log that rots."

He looked up quickly from his scavenger

hunt card. "I remember seeing a rotting log back that way!" He pointed to the other end of the museum and raced over to the glass display case.

Fiona, Madison and Andrew followed. They peered through the glass. A rotting log lay on a bed of moss.

"Do you see anything?" asked Madison.

"Nope."

"Just moss and rocks."

Daniel leaned in closer to the glass. Something was moving underneath the log. "What's that?" he asked.

Two beady black eyes blinked back at him. Before he could say anything, a dark grey thing slithered beneath some leaves. It moved super fast, but not fast enough to stop Daniel from seeing a bunch of yellow spots.

"I saw it!" he yelled. "I saw the yellow spots!"

"What was it?" asked Fiona.

Daniel looked up at the sign. The words "Yellow-Spotted Salamander" were written in thick black print.

"So I guess this is where the class is meeting for lunch," said Fiona.

Chapter 15

After lunch one of the museum guides invited the class to watch a demonstration called "This Museum Is Bugged." Fiona sat in the very front row next to Madison. Daniel stood near the back. He remembered reading that some insects could be dangerous, even poisonous. There was no way he was going anywhere near a tarantula. What if it bit him? And who knew what would happen if the giant African millipede got loose? It would probably crawl up his pant leg. Maybe get inside his underwear. The back row was a perfect spot to watch the bugs.

Daniel wasn't surprised that Fiona was the first person who volunteered to hold a hissing cockroach. Daniel watched as the eight-centimetre bug crawled over his sister's hand. He shuddered.

The demonstration was almost over when the museum guide looked toward the back of the room.

"Any of you kids at the back want to take a turn holding one of our bugs?" she asked. "Maybe a praying mantis or a stick bug? Or maybe your teacher or some of the chaperones would like to hold one?"

Ms. Belliveau smiled. "I'm happy just to watch," she answered.

"Me, too," replied Daniel.

"Well then, that wraps up your tour today," the museum guide told the class. "Thanks for coming. On your way out of the museum, you'll probably see Gus the gopher tortoise out for his daily walk. Don't forget to say hi to him. And remember to stop by our gift shop. You might want to buy some chocolate-covered crickets. They're absolutely bug-a-licious!"

Andrew turned to Daniel. He looked horrified. "Can you imagine eating crickets? That's gross!"

Daniel laughed. "Bet cricket soup would be even better. And cricket ice cream. Maybe cricket cookies!" He paused. "Yeah, you're right. Chocolate crickets would be gross. I'll stick to plain ol' chocolate."

"It was such a great day," said Andrew. "Do you know what would make this even better? A sleepover tonight! It would be so much fun!"

Daniel sighed. A sleepover. This was the

second time Andrew had asked him. He was pretty sure that if he didn't go soon, Andrew would stop inviting him. Deep down inside, Daniel knew he'd have fun right up until the time they had to go to sleep. But he still preferred to sleep with a night light, especially when he visited new places. What would Andrew think about that?

"Um . . . I'm not sure I can go," he said. "I'll have to ask my parents."

Andrew gave him a funny look. The bus ride back to school was pretty quiet.

Chapter 16

Back at the school, Ms. Belliveau began by saying, "So, that was a fun day! Would anyone like to share what he or she enjoyed the most? Maybe you even learned a few new facts for your presentation."

Just the mention of the word "presentation" made Daniel forget about all the fun he'd had at the museum. His eyebrows scrunched together. He still hadn't figured out which animal he wanted to research. Then he had to plan the actual presentation. That was a humongous worry. And the project needed to be finished by Monday.

Daniel thought back to when he was five years old. He had really wanted to learn how to snowboard. But he had worried he would fall and hurt himself. He worried he'd be embarrassed if he looked silly. Mostly he worried that he wouldn't be able to do it. Now he could snowboard on the biggest hills.

I can do this presentation, he thought. *If I take it one step at a time just like when I learned to snowboard.* Daniel remembered starting on little hills. Then moving to medium-sized hills. Finally he could snowboard on all the hills *and* do lots of really cool tricks.

He took a deep breath. The first step was deciding what to do his presentation on. The snakes at the museum were pretty interesting. So were the newts. He pulled his library books from his desk and began flipping through the pages. Halfway through the second book he paused. He stared at the photo. It was the perfect creepy crawly to do his project on. It all made sense now!

Ms. Belliveau gave the kids the last part of the day to work on their projects. Andrew sat next to Daniel. He was putting the finishing touches on his diorama. He fluffed the moss and placed a few stones in the corner of the shoebox. He watched as Daniel frantically jotted down information on sticky notes. "Looks like you finally decided what to do your project on," he said. "That's great!"

Daniel smiled.

"So," Andrew paused, "do you think your mom and dad will let you come over for a sleepover? We could play a little baseball. Maybe watch a movie . . ."

Daniel's smile slipped a notch. He pointed to the stickies on his desk. "Sorry, but I really think I need to work on this. I took too long to decide about my project."

The funny part was Daniel really meant it this time. But the look on Andrew's face said that he didn't believe his friend at all.

Chapter 17

Fiona raced off the bus when they got home. She couldn't wait to tell Mom that her project was finished. Her poster had glittery dragonflies and tons of cool facts. "Best of all," said Fiona, "I asked Ms. Belliveau if I could be the first person to do my presentation next week. And she said yes!"

It figures that Fiona would want to go first, thought Daniel. She wasn't nervous about standing in front of the whole class to give a presentation. She'd love every minute of it. *I wish I could be just a little bit like her,* he thought.

"That sounds great," said Mom. "What about you, Daniel? How's your project coming along?"

This time Daniel felt a little bit excited about his project. "Well," he answered, "it took me a long time to figure out what I wanted to do. I have a lot of information. Now I have to put it all together." He picked a hangnail on his thumb.

"That's great news!" said Mom.

Daniel looked at Mom, then Fiona. He spoke softly. "What if I can't speak, like last time?"

"That won't happen again," Mom said.

"Just have some sips of water before you go up," added Fiona. "And remember all the tips I gave you. You'll be great!" She studied her brother. "What's your project on, anyway?"

A small smile crept across Daniel's face. "It's going to be a surprise," he said.

* * *

Long after supper was over, Daniel worked on his project. His bedroom door was tightly shut. "You can't come in," he called out when Fiona knocked on his door.

"Who does school work on a Friday?" she asked. "And besides, Andrew is here to see you."

Daniel heard the *stomp-stomp* of Fiona's footsteps going down the hall.

I wonder why Andrew is here. It's kind of weird, he thought. He knew they didn't have any plans for that night. Or for the whole weekend. *Something must be up. But what?*

Andrew didn't look too happy to be sitting in the Coutures' living room. A small suitcase and a sleeping bag were on the floor next to him.

"Why are you here?" Daniel blurted out. "I thought I told you I had to work on my project this weekend."

Dad looked from Andrew to Daniel. "Well, it turns out that Andrew's parents had to make an emergency trip to the hospital. It seems Andrew is about to get a baby sister or brother a little earlier than expected. So he's going to stay with us for the night."

Dad smiled when he saw the look on Andrew's face. "Try not to worry. You'll be a big brother before you know it."

Daniel studied Andrew's face. He didn't just look worried. He looked scared. Daniel plopped down next to him. He put his arm around him. "Don't worry. Your mom and dad will be home soon." He paused before he added, "And then there'll be a crying baby with poopy diapers. The good news is — you'll be the oldest *and* the smartest. But best of all, you won't have to change stinky diapers!"

That made Andrew smile.

Chapter 18

Daniel and Andrew spent the next few hours making the best fort ever out of blankets, until Mom yelled, "Bedtime!" Then they dragged sleeping bags, a flashlight and Andrew's secret stash of gummi bears into the fort.

"They're not chocolate-covered crickets," he laughed. "But they're my favourite — especially the red ones!"

The fort was dark. Daniel thought about his night light — turned off on the other side of the room. He switched on the flashlight. "I think we should sleep with the light on in case you need to get a drink of water in the middle of the night," he said. And for good measure he added, "Because my room is really, really dark."

"Good idea," said Andrew. "At home I always sleep with a night light."

"You do?" asked Daniel. "Really?"

He thought about what Andrew had said. He didn't even care that someone else knew he slept with a night light.

Andrew was quiet for a long time. Then suddenly he whispered, "Did you hear that?"

"What?"

Then Daniel heard it, too. A noise was coming from the closet. Again. Daniel knew there was no such thing as ghosts. Or monsters that lived under his bed. But there *was* something in the closet. For real!

The sound was low. Then it grew louder and louder until "the thing" was clawing at the door. It was trying to escape!

"I want to go home," Andrew whispered. His eyes were big and round. His lower lip quivered.

But Andrew couldn't go home. There was no one there. His mom and dad were still at the hospital. So it was up to Daniel. He knew deep down inside that there was nothing bad in the closet. *I need to be brave — just this once. For Andrew,* he thought.

He unzipped his sleeping bag. He flipped back the blanket that was the door to the fort. His flashlight wobbled back and forth.

"Wh . . . wh . . . where are you going?" asked Andrew. His voice came out all squeaky.

Daniel took a deep breath. He swallowed hard. "I'm going to check out the noise."

Chapter 19

"Don't leave me here!" begged Andrew.

"*Shhh!* Then follow me," Daniel whispered. He tried to think of everything Mom and Dad had said about being brave, but he couldn't remember a single thing.

He crept closer to the closet. The noise was getting louder. Whatever "the thing" was — and it was definitely real, not a pretend monster — it was getting madder by the minute. He passed the flashlight to Andrew. Daniel swallowed hard. "You hold this while I open the door," he instructed. He reached over and picked up his plastic baseball bat. "I'll count to three," he said. "Then I'll open the door. Ready?"

Daniel had a hard time taking a deep breath. His heart was hammering in his chest.

"One. Two. Three!" he whispered. And he yanked open the door!

The inside of the closet was dark. Shadows seemed to move to the left and then to the right. The noise had stopped . . . for now. Then something grabbed Daniel's ankle!  He tried not to scream as he frantically shook "the thing" off his leg! But it wouldn't let go. It was attacking him!

Andrew shone the flashlight toward the floor. Two green eyes stared back at the boys. Glittery, evil eyes!

As quickly as "the thing" had grabbed hold of Daniel's leg, it let go. Then it pushed against him. It was soft and furry. "Mittens!" he exclaimed. He stared at the cat and scooped her up. He rubbed his face against her fur. "You scared us half to death!"

Andrew exhaled a long breath. "It was your

cat the whole time?" he laughed in a shaky voice. "Phew. I was sure it was a ghost."

* * *

Back in the fort, Mittens purred loudly between Daniel and Andrew.

"Does your cat always do such crazy things?" asked Andrew.

Daniel thought back to his seventh birthday. The time he picked out Mittens at the animal shelter. She *had* done some crazy things since then. Like the time she dragged in a dead mouse and dropped it on Mom's slippers, kind of like a present. Or like the time Daniel got his first guitar. Every time he tried to play a chord, Mittens meowed. Whenever Daniel stopped playing, she stopped meowing. Or last summer when she chased the biggest dog in the neighbourhood down the street! Yup. She was a crazy kitty.

He laughed. "Yeah, she does crazy stuff sometimes. But this was about the scariest. I'm glad I finally figured out what was making the noise in my closet. She'll be okay now that she's with us."

"You were really brave," said Andrew. "I don't think I would have looked in the closet. Ever. I'd be too scared."

Daniel stopped scratching Mittens's ears. Brave. Andrew had just called *him* brave. Even though he had been scared, Daniel had found the courage to open the door. It was a good feeling.

"Do . . . do . . . you think it would be all right for me to hold Mittens? Just until I fall asleep?" Andrew asked.

Daniel passed him the cat. "Sure," he said.

Five minutes later Andrew was snoring. The last thing Daniel heard before drifting off to sleep was Mittens's loud purr.

Chapter 20

Daniel opened his eyes to Dad's face peering into the fort. "Wake up, boys," he whispered. "Andrew, you're a big brother!"

Andrew rubbed the sleep from his eyes. "Really?"

"Yup. Your dad just called. You have a new baby sister. He's going to pick you up in a few minutes and take you to the hospital for a visit."

"That's awesome," said Daniel. He nudged Andrew in the arm when he added, "Now you'll find out how much fun little sisters can be!"

As soon as Andrew left, Daniel dragged out all the information he had for his project. He counted eleven stickies. That meant eleven really cool facts. He was beginning to feel like he would be an expert by Monday. But first he needed just a teeny little bit of help.

He could ask Fiona, but sometimes she got a little bossy. Besides, she was playing over at Madison's for the day. Since Mom was at her yoga class, that left Dad.

Dad listened carefully when Daniel explained how he needed his help.

"Okay," agreed Dad. "Let's do it!"

It took a lot longer than Daniel thought it would, but by suppertime, his presentation was ready. And even though Fiona begged to know all about it, Daniel would only smile. "You'll see on Monday," he said. He sounded very confident.

But on Monday morning, Daniel didn't feel confident at all. The butterflies in his belly were so bad he couldn't eat any breakfast. He thought about the tips Fiona had given him. He was pretty sure the kids would find his presentation interesting. He had practised in front of a mirror for a long time. Plus, he had a prop — well, sort of.

"Okay, you two, it's time to get ready for school," Mom said. She looked at Daniel. "I hear Dad's driving you today."

"Why?" asked Fiona. "Dad hardly ever drives us." She looked at Daniel, who didn't seem the least bit surprised. "What's going on? Does this have something to do with your presentation? Tell me," she begged.

But Daniel only smiled.

Fiona studied Daniel once she was in the car. "Where is your project? I don't see any posters or anything," she said.

"Right here," answered Daniel. He patted his backpack. "And the rest of it is in the trunk."

* * *

Of course Fiona went first with her presentation. Just like she said she would. Daniel tried to concentrate, but he was too nervous. He thought he heard her say that dragonflies have been around since the time of the dinosaurs. Or maybe she said dragonflies were related to dinosaurs. He just couldn't focus on what she was saying.

By the time Andrew did his presentation,

the butterflies in Daniel's belly were even worse. *I should go next and get it over with*, he thought.

So when Ms. Belliveau asked who would like to present next, Daniel surprised himself by raising his hand. "I can do this. I can do this," he whispered to himself.

He reached into his backpack for the memory stick that held his project. He felt on one side. Then the other. Nothing, unless you counted an empty granola bar wrapper!

Daniel paused. He knew he'd put the memory stick in his backpack last night. But where was it? Then he remembered — the secret compartment! Frantically he unzipped the hidden pouch. There it was — with one other very important item.

Phew! He breathed a sigh of relief and walked to the front of the class.

Chapter 21

"For a minute I thought I'd lost these." Daniel held up the memory stick and a small triangular piece of plastic. "That would have made my presentation a lot harder."

Daniel plugged the stick into the computer. He faced the class. Ms. Belliveau was smiling. Fiona gave him a thumbs-up signal. Daniel willed himself not to hiccup. He hoped his belly would be okay. He pictured the class sitting in their underwear. *I can do this*, he thought. He took a deep breath.

"Some of you know that I like to snowboard. But not many of you know that I really like music." He reached behind Ms. Belliveau's desk and pulled out . . . his guitar.

Daniel saw the surprised look on Fiona's

face. When their dad had dropped them off at school that morning, she'd run off to play on the swings with Madison and hadn't seen Daniel sneak into the school with the guitar.

"I like all kinds of music. In fact," he paused, "one of the first songs I learned to play was by a famous group with a creepy crawly name."

The class looked puzzled. Even Ms. Belliveau couldn't figure out what Daniel meant. Then Fiona blurted out, "The Beatles! You did your project on beetles!"

Daniel smiled. "Exactly. Now if everyone would watch the screen."

But the Grade Three class all stared at Daniel and his guitar. He used that triangular piece of plastic — his guitar pick — to strum a few chords. "I wrote some lyrics about beetles to one of my favourite tunes, called 'Love Me Do.' It's by an old group called . . . the Beatles. So, if you'll watch the pictures on the screen, I'll tell — er, I mean, sing — some interesting facts about beetles, the insects. Oh," he paused, "I had a bit of help from my Dad with some of the rhyming parts."

Music filled the classroom. All eyes were glued on Daniel, then on the screen, then back on Daniel. The minute he started to strum his guitar, Daniel felt calmer. He didn't need to picture  the kids sitting in their underwear. He wasn't the least bit worried about squeaking or hiccupping. He could do this. Pictures of leaf beetles and fireflies flashed across the screen. He sang:

Beetles are cool.
I learned this at school.
I know this is true.
These facts are for you.
Beetles are cool. Whoa, beetles are cool.

Beetles can be little,
The size of tiny dots.
They come in every colour.
Some even have black spots.
Beetles are cool. Whoa, beetles are cool.

Beetles live all over,
From forests to the plains,
In the desert where it's dry,
Or the wetland where it rains.

Beetles are insects.
Some can swim, crawl or fly.
Others burrow in the earth,
To keep eggs warm and dry.
Beetles are cool. Whoa, beetles are cool.

Beetles have a hardened shell,
Three separate body parts,
Six legs, two compound eyes.
They even have a heart.
Beetles are cool. Whoa, beetles are cool.

Beetles are amazing!
Some chirp and kind of sing.
Some even make a sound,
By rubbing wing to wing.

Beetles can be helpful.
For some this is *not* true.
I researched them for days,
And found facts I never knew!
Beetles are cool. Whoa, beetles are cool.

When he was finished strumming the last chord, a photo of a ladybug remained on the screen.

Then the most amazing thing happened. The entire class stood and applauded. Someone shouted, "Play another song!"

"You're a rock star!"

When Daniel took his seat, Andrew leaned over and whispered, "Can you teach me how to play the guitar?"

Daniel smiled. It seemed everyone loved the presentation!

Ms. Belliveau walked to the front of the room. "That was absolutely wonderful," she said. "Bravo!"

Daniel had to admit it *was* an amazing feeling to finally do something he had been afraid of for so long. He had been scared to stand in front of the class. Most of all, he had worried he would fail. But he, Daniel Couture, had conquered fear. He had been brave. True, he had been nervous at the beginning, but once he got started, he had rocked it! The next time he had to give a presentation, he wouldn't be worried. (Well, maybe a teeny bit, but it would only be for a little while.)

At that moment he realized last year's birthday wish had finally come true. Daniel had become braver. But best of all, next week he would be celebrating his ninth birthday. And that meant a brand new wish!

Chapter 22

Daniel dug through his lunch bag, looking for his dessert. Sure enough, Dad had packed his favourite — chocolate-covered raisins. They reminded him of the chocolate-covered crickets at the museum gift shop. Raisins were better. Way better. Tucked inside the bag was a note.

Dear Daniel,

Good luck giving your presentation. You will do a great job! Everyone will be amazed that you can play guitar!

Love,
Dad

Daniel popped a handful of raisins into his mouth.

Just then Andrew tapped him on the shoulder. "Hey," he said. "The Comedy Club meets today. Do you want to come?"

Daniel glanced down at his snack. He remembered the last time Andrew had asked him to join the club; the time he had been too scared to even try. That time he had eaten his raisins very *slooooowly.*

He held up his bag of raisins for Andrew to see. "I need to finish the rest of my lunch. Maybe later." Once again Daniel began to slowly eat his raisins one at a time. Except the raisins didn't taste very good. And he had a hard time swallowing them.

What if I don't do a good job telling my riddle? he thought. *What if no one finds it funny? What if . . .* Daniel took a deep breath and slowly exhaled. *Or . . . maybe I could tell an old riddle. One I know really well. I . . . might do an okay job.* He stuffed the leftover raisins in his lunch bag. He took another deep breath.

"I'll give it a try," he said. "I could tell a music riddle. So . . . do you know the difference between a guitar and a tuna fish?"

When Andrew shook his head, Daniel said, "You can tune a guitar but you can't tuna fish."

* * *

After lunchtime the kids in the Comedy Club walked back to their classrooms.

Andrew studied Daniel carefully. "I thought you said you weren't very good at jokes and riddles? You had everyone laughing today."

Daniel grinned. He felt amazing. The club had been a blast! He had laughed so hard that he had forgotten to be nervous about speaking to a group of people. And that's when he realized that he had done not one, but *two* things he had been afraid of doing — all in one day.

Before they reached the classroom, Andrew stopped walking. He had a look on his face that said he had something important on his mind.

After a few seconds, he blurted out, "I know I've asked you before, but do you think maybe this weekend you could come to my house for a sleepover? It would be lots of fun. You could even meet my new baby sister, Ella."

Daniel thought for a moment. He knew Andrew slept with a night light, just like him. All Daniel had to do was be brave and give it a try.

He smiled at Andrew. "That would be fun! I'll even bring my guitar. Maybe I could teach you how to play a song."